WOOF
AND THE
PAPER ROUTE

by Danae Dobson

Illustrated by Karen Loccisano

WORD PUBLISHING
Dallas·London·Vancouver·Melbourne

This book is dedicated to Rev. H.B. London, Jr.,
who is not only a member of my family
but also my pastor. He has encouraged me
and has been my friend.
Thank you, H.B.!

Woof and the Paper Route
Copyright © 1991 by Danae Dobson for the text. Copyright © 1991 by Karen Loccisano for the illustrations.

Library of Congress Cataloging-in-Publication Data

Dobson, Danae.
    Woof and the paper route / by Danae Dobson ; illustrated by Karen Loccisano.
        p.   cm. — (The Woof series ; 10)
    "Word kids!"
    Summary: Mark gets in trouble when the Harper twins steal the newspapers he delivers on his paper route, but Woof saves the day.
    ISBN 0-8499-0878-7
    [1. Newspaper carriers — Fiction.   2. Dogs — Fiction.
3. Christian life — Fiction.] I. Loccisano, Karen, ill. II. Title.
III. Series: Dobson, Danae. The Woof series ; 10.
PZ7.D6614Wrf 1991
[Fic] — dc20   90-28438
                                      CIP
                                       AC

Printed in the United States of America

1 2 3 4 5 6 9 AGH 9 8 7 6 5 4 3 2 1

A MESSAGE FROM
Dr. James Dobson

Before you read about this dog named Woof perhaps you would like to know how these books came to be written. When my children, Danae and Ryan, were young, I often told them stories at bedtime. Many of those tales were about pet animals who were loved by people like those in our own family. Later, I created more stories while driving the children to school in our car pool. The kids began to fall in love with these pets, even though they existed only in our minds. I found out just how much they loved these animals when I made the mistake of telling them a story in which one of their favorite pets died. There were so many tears I had to bring him back to life!

These tales made a special impression on Danae. At the age of twelve, she decided to write her own book about her favorite animal, Woof, and see if Word Publishers would like to print it. She did, and they did, and in the process she became the youngest author in Word's history. Now, thirteen years later, Danae has written nine more, totally new adventures with Woof and the Petersons. And she is still Word's youngest author!

Danae has discovered a talent God has given her, and it all started with our family spending time together, talking about a dog and the two children who loved him. We hope that not only will you enjoy Woof's adventures but that you and your family will enjoy the time spent reading them together. Perhaps you also will discover a talent God has given you.

Mark Peterson looked anxious as he followed his sister down the sidewalk.

"We have to hurry, Krissy," he said, stopping to tie his shoelace. "Mother told us to be home in an hour."

"I know," answered Krissy. "But we can't go home until we find a new collar for Woof. We made him a promise, and he'll be disappointed if we change our minds."

Mark looked down at Woof who was happily wagging his tail. "All right," he sighed. "But we don't have much time."

The Peterson children continued walking toward the pet shop.

Just then, something caught Mark's eye.

"Hey! Look at that!" Mark exclaimed, peering in a store window. "What a great bicycle! I'd really like to have one of those!"

"It's too expensive," said ten-year-old Krissy. "And you don't have any money."

Mark looked unhappy as he pressed his face against the window. "I guess I'll have to ask for it for my birthday," he said.

"But that's months from now," said Krissy. "Why don't you get a job and earn the money?"

Mark laughed at his sister. "I'm only six years old. How could I get a job?"

"Well," said Krissy, "how about a paper route? The boy who delivers newspapers in our neighborhood is moving away. The newspaper office is going to need someone to take his place. Maybe we could do the job together. I'd like some extra money, too. Besides, it's summer and we don't have to go to school."

"Wow! A paper route!" exclaimed Mark. "Let's ask Mom and Dad about it when we get home."

An hour later, Mark and Krissy returned home with Woof, who was wearing a bright, new collar.

"Why, it's lovely," said Mother, patting the shaggy-haired dog on the head. Woof panted and wagged his tail. He was just a mutt with a crooked leg and a bent tail. But the Peterson family loved him very much. To Mark and Krissy, he was the most wonderful dog in the world.

After lunch, the kids talked to their parents about starting a paper route. At first, Mr. and Mrs. Peterson didn't like the idea.

"It's a big responsibility," Father said. "And Mark is too young for it." But the two children promised to work hard and help each other.

"You'll have to get up early *every* morning and deliver the papers correctly. This is an important job," Mr. Peterson said.

"Okay," Krissy replied. "We can do it. I know we can."

"Please let us try," begged Mark. He was determined to get that new bicycle.

Mr. Peterson smiled and agreed to take them to the newspaper office.

Before long they arrived at *The Gladstone Press* to apply for the job. Mr. Thurman was in charge of the paper carriers. He was a gruff person with a deep voice. He explained how the paper routes worked. Krissy was old enough to have her own route, but Mark wasn't. Krissy asked if Mark could help her. Mr. Thurman said he could.

Then he reminded her that she would still be responsible for the route. Krissy said she would make sure everyone got a paper.

"Well . . ." said Mr. Thurman, "I guess I'll give you a try. But those papers must be delivered on time. Otherwise, I'll have to give the route to someone else."

Mark and Krissy were very excited when they returned home. "We got the job!" Mark exclaimed to Mother. "We start tomorrow."

For the rest of the afternoon, the children practiced with their father. Mr. Peterson took them around the neighborhood to find the correct addresses. Mark and Krissy worked out a plan for dividing the route. Mark would have the 25 houses closest to home, and Krissy would have the rest.

Early the next morning, *The Gladstone Press*
delivered 50 newspapers to the Peterson home. Mark and
Krissy divided them evenly. Krissy put her papers in her
bicycle basket, and Mark put his in the wagon. Then off
they went in different directions. Mark called for Woof to
follow him.

Mark was very careful about delivering all the
papers. He wanted his parents and sister to be proud
of him.

But later that afternoon, Krissy received a telephone call from Mr. Thurman. He was very angry. Half the people on the route had not received their papers. They were the ones Mark delivered papers to.

"What happened? Mr. Thurman asked. "Did you forget those houses?"

"I-I-don't know," answered Krissy. "We were very careful . . ."

"Well, you did *something* wrong," interrupted Mr. Thurman. "I know this was your first day, but you must be more careful. If this happens again, I'll have to give the route to someone else."

"Yes sir," answered Krissy, hanging up the receiver. "Mark!" she called out. "What did you do? No one on your half of the paper route got a newspaper!"

Mark was confused. "That couldn't have happened," he said. "I know I delivered them all . . ."

Just then Mother walked in to take a pie out of the oven. "What's wrong?" she asked, seeing the sad look on both their faces.

"That was Mr. Thurman on the phone. He said 25 people didn't get their newspapers this morning. All of them are on Mark's part of the route," Krissy explained. She was trying not to cry.

"I know I did it right," Mark insisted. "I was very careful to deliver them to each house."

Mother sighed. "Well, try to be even *more* careful tomorrow. Mr. Thurman doesn't want to lose his customers, you know."

The following morning Krissy, Mark, and Woof set out to deliver papers again. This time Mark was *extremely* cautious! He watched Woof carry a paper to the front porch of every house. It took longer this way, but Mark didn't want to lose the job. It was very important to him. He also didn't want his sister to get in trouble.

At one point, Woof sensed they were being followed. He turned to look behind him, but didn't see anyone.

That afternoon Krissy received another call from Mr. Thurman. This time, he was even more upset than before.

"Krissy, it happened again! The people on half of your route didn't get their papers. Eight of them have canceled. I'm sorry, but I'll have to give the job to someone else."

Krissy couldn't believe what was happening. Just then, Mark came into the room. "Mark, you've done it again!" she cried. "Mr. Thurman just called. The same houses didn't get a paper again today. He's giving our route to someone else." Krissy ran to her room sobbing. Mark felt terrible. He knew he had done everything he was told to do.

Just then a furry head peeked around the doorway. It was Woof. He walked over to his special friend and licked his hand.

"I don't understand what went wrong," cried Mark. He reached down to stroke Woof's fur. "I tried to do my best."

Woof curled up at Mark's feet and sighed. He loved Mark and didn't like to see him sad. He wished there was something he could do.

When the rest of the family learned what happened, they felt bad, also.

"It's my fault," said Father. "I should have helped you deliver the papers the first few days." Then he suggested they go out for ice cream.

As the family was getting into the car, Woof wandered next-door. He thought he smelled food scraps in a nearby trash can. But then he saw it! He couldn't believe his eyes. It was a wagon filled with Mark's newspapers! He wondered what they were doing there. Then he remembered who lived next-door. "The mean bullies, Billy and Bobby Harper! They must have stolen Mark's papers!" Woof thought.

"Woof! Here boy!" called Mr. Peterson.

Woof ran back to the family and barked. He was trying to make them understand. But no one paid any attention to him. Woof was still barking as he got in the car.

"Shh," said Krissy. "Calm down, will you?"

Woof was very upset on the way to the ice cream shop. He *had* to make the family understand what he had seen.

Just then, the Peterson car turned onto Raymond Street. There on the corner were Billy and Bobby Harper! They were selling newspapers for 25 cents a piece! Woof began to bark and jump all over the seats.

"What's the matter with this crazy dog?" asked Mother, brushing the paw marks off her skirt.

"He probably saw a cat or — Look!" Krissy shouted. "That's Billy and Bobby Harper!"

Mark gasped. "They don't have a paper route! I'll bet those newspapers are mine!"

"You're probably right," agreed Father. "I don't think the company allows anyone to sell papers on the street. We'd better go report it."

The family quickly drove to *The Gladstone Press.* When they got there, Mr. Thurman was leaving the building. Mark and Krissy jumped out of the car and ran to meet him.

Mr. Thurman saw them and stopped.

"I'm sorry, kids, but you can't keep the paper route."

"Please listen," said Krissy. "Should anyone be selling newspapers on Raymond Street?

"Why, no," answered Mr. Thurman. "Nobody sells papers, they're delivered door-to-door."

Krissy quickly explained the story as Father walked over and joined them.

"It sounds like these boys are up to some mischief," said Mr. Thurman. "Why don't I follow you over there? I want to see what's going on."

Soon the two cars came to a stop on Raymond Street. Mr. Thurman wasted no time in getting out of his car. He went over to Billy and Bobby.

"What do you boys think you're doing?" he said.

"Who are *you*?" asked Bobby, very rudely.

"I'm the supervisor of *The Gladstone Press*," answered Mr. Thurman. He leaned down to look them in the eye. "Where did you boys get these papers?"

Billy and Bobby both gulped. "We found them," Bobby said.

"Well, I better not ever catch you messing with my papers again! Next time just leave them exactly where you found them. If you ever do this again I will call the police. Now go home."

The twins ran past the Petersons and down the street.

"I don't think they'll try that again," said Mr. Thurman. He carried the newspapers to the trunk of his car.

"Krissy, I'm very sorry," said Mr. Thurman. "I was wrong about you. You may keep the paper route.

Come by my office Monday morning. There's a $100
reward for helping catch people who steal our papers."

Krissy smiled and shook hands with the supervisor.
"Thank you," she said. "We'll be there!"

Mr. Thurman said good-bye to the Petersons and
drove down the street.

"I'm sorry I didn't believe you, Mark," said Krissy. "I want you to have half of the reward."

"Wow!" exclaimed Mark, "Thank you! Now I can buy the new bicycle!"

"Krissy, what are you going to spend your money on?" asked Mother.

Krissy thought for a moment. "I guess I'll save it until there's something I really want," she said.

The next day was Sunday, so the Petersons went to church. Their pastor talked about a very important verse in the Bible.

It was Numbers 32:23 which says: "your sin will find you out." Pastor Reeves explained this scripture. He said some people do bad things and think no one will ever know. But sin is very hard to hide. Even if people never learn about your secret, God is always watching. We can never hide anything from Him! That is why it's so important to obey God.

Krissy leaned over and whispered in Mark's ear. "That's just what happened to the Harper twins. They didn't think they would get caught, but they did."

Mark nodded in agreement.

The next morning, Krissy and Mark delivered all the papers around their neighborhood. Then the family drove to the shop to buy Mark's new bicycle. There it was in the window — all shiny and beautiful. The young boy felt proud as the manager set the bike in front of him. Mark climbed on and rode right out the door.

"Now I have a bicycle for the paper route," he exclaimed. It was a happy moment for Mark. He waved to his parents as he followed their car down the street — with Woof running closely behind.